SELECTED POEMS

T. S. ELIOT

SELECTED POEMS

T. S. ELIOT

Selected Poems

By

T. S. Eliot

To Jean Verdenal 1889-1915

Certain of these poems first appeared in Poetry, Blast, Others, The Little Review, and Art and Letters.

Contents

Poems

Gerontion

Thou hast nor youth nor age

But as it were an after dinner sleep

Dreaming of both.

Here I am, an old man in a dry month,

Being read to by a boy, waiting for rain.

I was neither at the hot gates

Nor fought in the warm rain

Nor knee deep in the salt marsh, heaving a cutlass,

Bitten by flies, fought.

My house is a decayed house,

And the jew squats on the window sill, the owner,

Spawned in some estaminet of Antwerp,

Blistered in Brussels, patched and peeled in London.

The goat coughs at night in the field overhead;

Rocks, moss, stonecrop, iron, merds.

The woman keeps the kitchen, makes tea,

Sneezes at evening, poking the peevish gutter.

      I an old man,

A dull head among windy spaces.

Signs are taken for wonders. "We would see a sign":

The word within a word, unable to speak a word,

Swaddled with darkness. In the juvescence of the year

Came Christ the tiger

In depraved May, dogwood and chestnut, flowering Judas,

To be eaten, to be divided, to be drunk

Among whispers; by Mr. Silvero

With caressing hands, at Limoges

Who walked all night in the next room;

By Hakagawa, bowing among the Titians;

By Madame de Tornquist, in the dark room

Shifting the candles; Fraulein von Kulp

Who turned in the hall, one hand on the door. Vacant shuttles

Weave the wind. I have no ghosts,

An old man in a draughty house

Under a windy knob.

After such knowledge, what forgiveness? Think now

History has many cunning passages, contrived corridors

And issues, deceives with whispering ambitions,

Guides us by vanities. Think now

She gives when our attention is distracted

And what she gives, gives with such supple confusions

That the giving famishes the craving. Gives too late

What's not believed in, or if still believed,

In memory only, reconsidered passion. Gives too soon

Into weak hands, what's thought can be dispensed with

Till the refusal propagates a fear. Think

Neither fear nor courage saves us. Unnatural vices

Are fathered by our heroism. Virtues

Are forced upon us by our impudent crimes.

These tears are shaken from the wrath-bearing tree.

The tiger springs in the new year. Us he devours. Think at last

We have not reached conclusion, when I

Stiffen in a rented house. Think at last

I have not made this show purposelessly

And it is not by any concitation

Of the backward devils.

I would meet you upon this honestly.

I that was near your heart was removed therefrom

To lose beauty in terror, terror in inquisition.

I have lost my passion: why should I need to keep it

Since what is kept must be adulterated?

I have lost my sight, smell, hearing, taste and touch:

How should I use it for your closer contact?

These with a thousand small deliberations

Protract the profit of their chilled delirium,

Excite the membrane, when the sense has cooled,

With pungent sauces, multiply variety

In a wilderness of mirrors. What will the spider do,

Suspend its operations, will the weevil

Delay? De Bailhache, Fresca, Mrs. Cammel, whirled

Beyond the circuit of the shuddering Bear

In fractured atoms. Gull against the wind, in the windy straits

Of Belle Isle, or running on the Horn,

White feathers in the snow, the Gulf claims,

And an old man driven by the Trades

To a sleepy corner.

      Tenants of the house,

Thoughts of a dry brain in a dry season.

Burbank with a Baedeker: Bleistein with a Cigar

Tra-la-la-la-la-la-laire—nil nisi divinum stabile

est; caetera fumus—the gondola stopped, the old

palace was there, how charming its grey and pink—

goats and monkeys, with such hair too!—so the

countess passed on until she came through the

little park, where Niobe presented her with a

cabinet, and so departed.

Burbank crossed a little bridge

Descending at a small hotel;

Princess Volupine arrived,

They were together, and he fell.

Defunctive music under sea

Passed seaward with the passing bell

Slowly: the God Hercules

Had left him, that had loved him well.

The horses, under the axletree

Beat up the dawn from Istria

With even feet. Her shuttered barge

Burned on the water all the day.

But this or such was Bleistein's way:

A saggy bending of the knees

And elbows, with the palms turned out,

Chicago Semite Viennese.

A lustreless protrusive eye
Stares from the protozoic slime
At a perspective of Canaletto.
The smoky candle end of time

Declines. On the Rialto once.
The rats are underneath the piles.
The jew is underneath the lot.
Money in furs. The boatman smiles,

Princess Volupine extends
A meagre, blue-nailed, phthisic hand
To climb the waterstair. Lights, lights,
She entertains Sir Ferdinand

Klein. Who clipped the lion's wings
And flea'd his rump and pared his claws?
Thought Burbank, meditating on
Time's ruins, and the seven laws.

Sweeney Erect

And the trees about me,
Let them be dry and leafless; let the rocks
Groan with continual surges; and behind me
Make all a desolation. Look, look, wenches!

Paint me a cavernous waste shore
Cast in the unstilted Cyclades,
Paint me the bold anfractuous rocks
Faced by the snarled and yelping seas.

Display me Aeolus above
Reviewing the insurgent gales
Which tangle Ariadne's hair
And swell with haste the perjured sails.

Morning stirs the feet and hands
(Nausicaa and Polypheme),
Gesture of orang-outang
Rises from the sheets in steam.

This withered root of knots of hair
Slitted below and gashed with eyes,
This oval O cropped out with teeth:
The sickle motion from the thighs

Jackknifes upward at the knees

Then straightens out from heel to hip

Pushing the framework of the bed

And clawing at the pillow slip.

Sweeney addressed full length to shave

Broadbottomed, pink from nape to base,

Knows the female temperament

And wipes the suds around his face.

(The lengthened shadow of a man

Is history, said Emerson

Who had not seen the silhouette

Of Sweeney straddled in the sun).

Tests the razor on his leg

Waiting until the shriek subsides.

The epileptic on the bed

Curves backward, clutching at her sides.

The ladies of the corridor

Find themselves involved, disgraced,

Call witness to their principles

And deprecate the lack of taste

Observing that hysteria

Might easily be misunderstood;

Mrs. Turner intimates

It does the house no sort of good.

But Doris, towelled from the bath,

Enters padding on broad feet,

Bringing sal volatile

And a glass of brandy neat.

A Cooking Egg

En l'an trentiesme de mon aage

  Que toutes mes hontes j'ay beues...

Pipit sate upright in her chair

  Some distance from where I was sitting;

Views of the Oxford Colleges

  Lay on the table, with the knitting.

Daguerreotypes and silhouettes,

  Her grandfather and great great aunts,

Supported on the mantelpiece

  An Invitation to the Dance.

. . . . . .

I shall not want Honour in Heaven

  For I shall meet Sir Philip Sidney

And have talk with Coriolanus

  And other heroes of that kidney.

I shall not want Capital in Heaven

  For I shall meet Sir Alfred Mond:

We two shall lie together, lapt

  In a five per cent Exchequer Bond.

I shall not want Society in Heaven,

  Lucretia Borgia shall be my Bride;

Her anecdotes will be more amusing

Than Pipit's experience could provide.

I shall not want Pipit in Heaven:
  Madame Blavatsky will instruct me
In the Seven Sacred Trances;
  Piccarda de Donati will conduct me.

.   .   .   .   .   .

But where is the penny world I bought
  To eat with Pipit behind the screen?
The red-eyed scavengers are creeping
  From Kentish Town and Golder's Green;

Where are the eagles and the trumpets?

  Buried beneath some snow-deep Alps.
Over buttered scones and crumpets
  Weeping, weeping multitudes
Droop in a hundred A.B.C.'s

["ABC's" signifes endemic teashops, found in all parts of
London. The initials signify "Aerated Bread Company,
Limited."—Project Gutenberg Editor's replacement of
original footnote]

Le Directeur

Malheur à la malheureuse Tamise!

Tamise! Qui coule si pres du Spectateur.

Le directeur

Conservateur

Du Spectateur

Empeste la brise.

Les actionnaires

Réactionnaires

Du Spectateur

Conservateur

Bras dessus bras dessous

Font des tours

A pas de loup.

Dans un égout

Une petite fille

En guenilles

Camarde

Regarde

Le directeur

Du Spectateur

Conservateur

Et crève d'amour.

Mélange adultère de tout

En Amerique, professeur;

En Angleterre, journaliste;

C'est à grands pas et en sueur

Que vous suivrez à peine ma piste.

En Yorkshire, conferencier;

A Londres, un peu banquier,

Vous me paierez bien la tête.

C'est à Paris que je me coiffe

Casque noir de jemenfoutiste.

En Allemagne, philosophe

Surexcité par Emporheben

Au grand air de Bergsteigleben;

J'erre toujours de-ci de-là

A divers coups de tra la la

De Damas jusqu'à Omaha.

Je celebrai mon jour de fête

Dans une oasis d'Afrique

Vêtu d'une peau de girafe.

On montrera mon cénotaphe

Aux côtes brûlantes de Mozambique.

Lune de Miel

Ils ont vu les Pays-Bas, ils rentrent à Terre Haute;

Mais une nuit d'été, les voici à Ravenne,

A l'sur le dos écartant les genoux

De quatre jambes molles tout gonflées de morsures.

On relève le drap pour mieux égratigner.

Moins d'une lieue d'ici est Saint Apollinaire

In Classe, basilique connue des amateurs

De chapitaux d'acanthe que touraoie le vent.

Ils vont prendre le train de huit heures

Prolonger leurs misères de Padoue à Milan

Ou se trouvent le Cène, et un restaurant pas cher.

Lui pense aux pourboires, et redige son bilan.

Ils auront vu la Suisse et traversé la France.

Et Saint Apollinaire, raide et ascétique,

Vieille usine désaffectée de Dieu, tient encore

Dans ses pierres ècroulantes la forme precise de Byzance.

The Hippopotamus

Similiter et omnes revereantur Diaconos, ut
mandatum Jesu Christi; et Episcopum, ut Jesum
Christum, existentem filium Patris; Presbyteros
autem, ut concilium Dei et conjunctionem
Apostolorum. Sine his Ecclesia non vocatur; de
quibus suadeo vos sic habeo.

S. IGNATII AD TRALLIANOS.

And when this epistle is read among you, cause
that it be read also in the church of the
Laodiceans.

The broad-backed hippopotamus
Rests on his belly in the mud;
Although he seems so firm to us
He is merely flesh and blood.

Flesh-and-blood is weak and frail,
Susceptible to nervous shock;
While the True Church can never fail
For it is based upon a rock.

The hippo's feeble steps may err
In compassing material ends,
While the True Church need never stir

To gather in its dividends.

The 'potamus can never reach
The mango on the mango-tree;
But fruits of pomegranate and peach
Refresh the Church from over sea.

At mating time the hippo's voice
Betrays inflexions hoarse and odd,
But every week we hear rejoice
The Church, at being one with God.

The hippopotamus's day
Is passed in sleep; at night he hunts;
God works in a mysterious way-
The Church can sleep and feed at once.

I saw the 'potamus take wing
Ascending from the damp savannas,
And quiring angels round him sing
The praise of God, in loud hosannas.

Blood of the Lamb shall wash him clean
And him shall heavenly arms enfold,
Among the saints he shall be seen
Performing on a harp of gold.

He shall be washed as white as snow,

By all the martyr'd virgins kiss,

While the True Church remains below

Wrapt in the old miasmal mist.

Dans le Restaurant

Le garcon délabré qui n'a rien à faire

Que de se gratter les doigts et se pencher sur mon épaule:

"Dans mon pays il fera temps pluvieux,

Du vent, du grand soleil, et de la pluie;

C'est ce qu'on appelle le jour de lessive des gueux."

(Bavard, baveux, à la croupe arrondie,

Je te prie, au moins, ne bave pas dans la soupe).

"Les saules trempés, et des bourgeons sur les ronces—

C'est là, dans une averse, qu'on s'abrite.

J'avais septtans, elle était plus petite.

Elle etait toute mouillée, je lui ai donné des primavères."

Les tâches de son gilet montent au chiffre de trente-huit.

"Je la chatouillais, pour la faire rire.

J'éprouvais un instant de puissance et de délire."

Mais alors, vieux lubrique, a cet âge...

"Monsieur, le fait est dur.

Il est venu, nous peloter, un gros chien;

Moi j'avais peur, je l'ai quittee a mi-chemin.

C'est dommage."

Mais alors, tu as ton vautour!

Va t'en te décrotter les rides du visage;

Tiens, ma fourchette, décrasse-toi le crâne.

De quel droit payes-tu des expériences comme moi?

Tiens, voilà dix sous, pour la salle-de-bains.

Phlébas, le Phénicien, pendant quinze jours noyé,

Oubliait les cris des mouettes et la houle de Cornouaille,

Et les profits et les pertes, et la cargaison d'etain:

Un courant de sous-mer l'emporta tres loin,

Le repassant aux étapes de sa vie antérieure.

Figurez-vous donc, c'etait un sort penible;

Cependant, ce fut jadis un bel homme, de haute taille.

Whispers of Immortality

Webster was much possessed by death

And saw the skull beneath the skin;

And breastless creatures under ground

Leaned backward with a lipless grin.

Daffodil bulbs instead of balls

Stared from the sockets of the eyes!

He knew that thought clings round dead limbs

Tightening its lusts and luxuries.

Donne, I suppose, was such another

Who found no substitute for sense;

To seize and clutch and penetrate,

Expert beyond experience,

He knew the anguish of the marrow

The ague of the skeleton;

No contact possible to flesh

Allayed the fever of the bone.

.   .   .   .   .

Grishkin is nice: her Russian eye

Is underlined for emphasis;

Uncorseted, her friendly bust

Gives promise of pneumatic bliss.

The couched Brazilian jaguar

Compels the scampering marmoset

With subtle effluence of cat;

Grishkin has a maisonette;

The sleek Brazilian jaguar

Does not in its arboreal gloom

Distil so rank a feline smell

As Grishkin in a drawing-room.

And even the Abstract Entities

Circumambulate her charm;

But our lot crawls between dry ribs

To keep our metaphysics warm.

Mr. Eliot's Sunday Morning Service

Look, look, master, here comes two religious

caterpillars.

       The Jew of Malta.

Polyphiloprogenitive

The sapient sutlers of the Lord

Drift across the window-panes.

In the beginning was the Word.

In the beginning was the Word.

Superfetation of [Greek text inserted here],

And at the mensual turn of time

Produced enervate Origen.

A painter of the Umbrian school

Designed upon a gesso ground

The nimbus of the Baptized God.

The wilderness is cracked and browned

But through the water pale and thin

Still shine the unoffending feet

And there above the painter set

The Father and the Paraclete.

. . . . .

The sable presbyters approach

The avenue of penitence;

The young are red and pustular
Clutching piaculative pence.

Under the penitential gates
Sustained by staring Seraphim
Where the souls of the devout
Burn invisible and dim.

Along the garden-wall the bees
With hairy bellies pass between
The staminate and pistilate,
Blest office of the epicene.

Sweeney shifts from ham to ham
Stirring the water in his bath.
The masters of the subtle schools
Are controversial, polymath.

Sweeney Among the Nightingales

Apeneck Sweeney spreads his knees
Letting his arms hang down to laugh,
The zebra stripes along his jaw
Swelling to maculate giraffe.

The circles of the stormy moon
Slide westward toward the River Plate,
Death and the Raven drift above
And Sweeney guards the hornèd gate.

Gloomy Orion and the Dog
Are veiled; and hushed the shrunken seas;
The person in the Spanish cape
Tries to sit on Sweeney's knees

Slips and pulls the table cloth
Overturns a coffee-cup,
Reorganized upon the floor
She yawns and draws a stocking up;

The silent man in mocha brown
Sprawls at the window-sill and gapes;
The waiter brings in oranges
Bananas figs and hothouse grapes;

The silent vertebrate in brown

Contracts and concentrates, withdraws;

Rachel née Rabinovitch

Tears at the grapes with murderous paws;

She and the lady in the cape

Are suspect, thought to be in league;

Therefore the man with heavy eyes

Declines the gambit, shows fatigue,

Leaves the room and reappears

Outside the window, leaning in,

Branches of wisteria

Circumscribe a golden grin;

The host with someone indistinct

Converses at the door apart,

The nightingales are singing near

The Convent of the Sacred Heart,

And sang within the bloody wood

When Agamemnon cried aloud,

And let their liquid droppings fall

To stain the stiff dishonoured shroud.

The Love Song of J. Alfred Prufrock

S'io credesse che mia risposta fosse

A persona che mai tornasse al mondo,

Questa fiamma staria senza piu scosse.

Ma perciocche giammai di questo fondo

Non torno vivo alcun, s'i'odo il vero,

Senza tema d'infamia ti rispondo.

Let us go then, you and I,

When the evening is spread out against the sky

Like a patient etherized upon a table;

Let us go, through certain half-deserted streets,

The muttering retreats

Of restless nights in one-night cheap hotels

And sawdust restaurants with oyster-shells:

Streets that follow like a tedious argument

Of insidious intent

To lead you to an overwhelming question....

Oh, do not ask, "What is it?"

Let us go and make our visit.

In the room the women come and go

Talking of Michelangelo.

The yellow fog that rubs its back upon the window-panes,

The yellow smoke that rubs its muzzle on the window-panes

Licked its tongue into the corners of the evening,

Lingered upon the pools that stand in drains,

Let fall upon its back the soot that falls from chimneys,

Slipped by the terrace, made a sudden leap,

And seeing that it was a soft October night,

Curled once about the house, and fell asleep.

And indeed there will be time

For the yellow smoke that slides along the street,

Rubbing its back upon the window panes;

There will be time, there will be time

To prepare a face to meet the faces that you meet

There will be time to murder and create,

And time for all the works and days of hands

That lift and drop a question on your plate;

Time for you and time for me,

And time yet for a hundred indecisions,

And for a hundred visions and revisions,

Before the taking of a toast and tea.

In the room the women come and go

Talking of Michelangelo.

And indeed there will be time

To wonder, "Do I dare?" and, "Do I dare?"

Time to turn back and descend the stair,

With a bald spot in the middle of my hair—

(They will say: "How his hair is growing thin!")

My morning coat, my collar mounting firmly to the chin,

My necktie rich and modest, but asserted by a simple pin—

(They will say: "But how his arms and legs are thin!")

Do I dare

Disturb the universe?

In a minute there is time

For decisions and revisions which a minute will reverse.

For I have known them all already, known them all:

Have known the evenings, mornings, afternoons,

I have measured out my life with coffee spoons;

I know the voices dying with a dying fall

Beneath the music from a farther room.

 So how should I presume?

And I have known the eyes already, known them all—

The eyes that fix you in a formulated phrase,

And when I am formulated, sprawling on a pin,

When I am pinned and wriggling on the wall,

Then how should I begin

To spit out all the butt-ends of my days and ways?

 And how should I presume?

And I have known the arms already, known them all—

Arms that are braceleted and white and bare

(But in the lamplight, downed with light brown hair!)

Is it perfume from a dress

That makes me so digress?

Arms that lie along a table, or wrap about a shawl.

  And should I then presume?

  And how should I begin?

. . . .

Shall I say, I have gone at dusk through narrow streets

And watched the smoke that rises from the pipes

Of lonely men in shirt-sleeves, leaning out of windows?

I should have been a pair of ragged claws

Scuttling across the doors of silent seas.

. . . .

And the afternoon, the evening, sleeps so peacefully!

Smoothed by long fingers,

Asleep... tired... or it malingers.

Stretched on on the floor, here beside you and me.

Should I, after tea and cakes and ices,

Have the strength to force the moment to its crisis?

But though I have wept and fasted, wept and prayed,

Though I have seen my head (grown slightly bald) brought in upon a platter,

I am no prophet—and here's no great matter;

I have seen the moment of my greatness flicker,

And I have seen the eternal Footman hold my coat, and snicker,

And in short, I was afraid.

And would it have been worth it, after all,

After the cups, the marmalade, the tea,

Among the porcelain, among some talk of you and me,

Would it have been worth while,

To have bitten off the matter with a smile,

To have squeezed the universe into a ball

To roll it toward some overwhelming question,

To say: "I am Lazarus, come from the dead,

Come back to tell you all, I shall tell you all"—

If one, settling a pillow by her head,

  Should say: "That is not what I meant at all;

  That is not it, at all."

And would it have been worth it, after all,

Would it have been worth while,

After the sunsets and the dooryards and the sprinkled streets,

After the novels, after the teacups, after the skirts that trail along the

    floor—

And this, and so much more?—

It is impossible to say just what I mean!

But as if a magic lantern threw the nerves in patterns on a screen:

Would it have been worth while

If one, settling a pillow or throwing off a shawl,

And turning toward the window, should say:

"That is not it at all,

That is not what I meant, at all."

.   .   .   .

No! I am not Prince Hamlet, nor was meant to be;

Am an attendant lord, one that will do

To swell a progress, start a scene or two,

Advise the prince; no doubt, an easy tool,

Deferential, glad to be of use,

Politic, cautious, and meticulous;

Full of high sentence, but a bit obtuse;

At times, indeed, almost ridiculous—

Almost, at times, the Fool.

I grow old... I grow old...

I shall wear the bottoms of my trousers rolled.

Shall I part my hair behind? Do I dare to eat a peach?

I shall wear white flannel trousers, and walk upon the beach.

I have heard the mermaids singing, each to each.

I do not think that they will sing to me.

I have seen them riding seaward on the waves

Combing the white hair of the waves blown back

When the wind blows the water white and black.

We have lingered in the chambers of the sea

By sea-girls wreathed with seaweed red and brown

Till human voices wake us, and we drown.

Portrait of a Lady

Thou hast committed—

Fornication: but that was in another country

And besides, the wench is dead.

The Jew of Malta.

I

Among the smoke and fog of a December afternoon

You have the scene arrange itself—as it will seem to do—

With "I have saved this afternoon for you";

And four wax candles in the darkened room,

Four rings of light upon the ceiling overhead,

An atmosphere of Juliet's tomb

Prepared for all the things to be said, or left unsaid.

We have been, let us say, to hear the latest Pole

Transmit the Preludes, through his hair and finger-tips.

"So intimate, this Chopin, that I think his soul

Should be resurrected only among friends

Some two or three, who will not touch the bloom

That is rubbed and questioned in the concert room."

—And so the conversation slips

Among velleities and carefully caught regrets

Through attenuated tones of violins

Mingled with remote cornets

And begins.

"You do not know how much they mean to me, my friends,

And how, how rare and strange it is, to find

In a life composed so much, so much of odds and ends,

(For indeed I do not love it... you knew? you are not blind!

How keen you are!)

To find a friend who has these qualities,

Who has, and gives

Those qualities upon which friendship lives.

How much it means that I say this to you—

Without these friendships—life, what cauchemar!"

Among the windings of the violins

And the ariettes

Of cracked cornets

Inside my brain a dull tom-tom begins

Absurdly hammering a prelude of its own,

Capricious monotone

That is at least one definite "false note."

—Let us take the air, in a tobacco trance,

Admire the monuments

Discuss the late events,

Correct our watches by the public clocks.

Then sit for half an hour and drink our bocks.

II

Now that lilacs are in bloom

She has a bowl of lilacs in her room

And twists one in her fingers while she talks.

"Ah, my friend, you do not know, you do not know

What life is, you should hold it in your hands";

(Slowly twisting the lilac stalks)

"You let it flow from you, you let it flow,

And youth is cruel, and has no remorse

And smiles at situations which it cannot see."

I smile, of course,

And go on drinking tea.

"Yet with these April sunsets, that somehow recall

My buried life, and Paris in the Spring,

I feel immeasurably at peace, and find the world

To be wonderful and youthful, after all."

The voice returns like the insistent out-of-tune

Of a broken violin on an August afternoon:

"I am always sure that you understand

My feelings, always sure that you feel,

Sure that across the gulf you reach your hand.

You are invulnerable, you have no Achilles' heel.

You will go on, and when you have prevailed

You can say: at this point many a one has failed.

But what have I, but what have I, my friend,

To give you, what can you receive from me?

Only the friendship and the sympathy

Of one about to reach her journey's end.

I shall sit here, serving tea to friends...."

I take my hat: how can I make a cowardly amends

For what she has said to me?

You will see me any morning in the park

Reading the comics and the sporting page.

Particularly I remark An English countess goes upon the stage.

A Greek was murdered at a Polish dance,

Another bank defaulter has confessed.

I keep my countenance, I remain self-possessed

Except when a street piano, mechanical and tired

Reiterates some worn-out common song

With the smell of hyacinths across the garden

Recalling things that other people have desired.

Are these ideas right or wrong?

III

The October night comes down; returning as before

Except for a slight sensation of being ill at ease

I mount the stairs and turn the handle of the door

And feel as if I had mounted on my hands and knees.

"And so you are going abroad; and when do you return?

But that's a useless question.

You hardly know when you are coming back,

You will find so much to learn."

My smile falls heavily among the bric-à-brac.

"Perhaps you can write to me."

My self-possession flares up for a second;

This is as I had reckoned.

"I have been wondering frequently of late

(But our beginnings never know our ends!)

Why we have not developed into friends."

I feel like one who smiles, and turning shall remark

Suddenly, his expression in a glass.

My self-possession gutters; we are really in the dark.

"For everybody said so, all our friends,

They all were sure our feelings would relate

So closely! I myself can hardly understand.

We must leave it now to fate.

You will write, at any rate.

Perhaps it is not too late.

I shall sit here, serving tea to friends."

And I must borrow every changing shape

To find expression... dance, dance

Like a dancing bear,

Cry like a parrot, chatter like an ape.

Let us take the air, in a tobacco trance—

Well! and what if she should die some afternoon,

Afternoon grey and smoky, evening yellow and rose;

Should die and leave me sitting pen in hand

With the smoke coming down above the housetops;

Doubtful, for quite a while

Not knowing what to feel or if I understand

Or whether wise or foolish, tardy or too soon...

Would she not have the advantage, after all?

This music is successful with a "dying fall"

Now that we talk of dying—

And should I have the right to smile?

Preludes

I

The winter evening settles down
With smell of steaks in passageways.
Six o'clock.
The burnt-out ends of smoky days.
And now a gusty shower wraps
The grimy scraps
Of withered leaves about your feet
And newspapers from vacant lots;
The showers beat
On broken blinds and chimney-pots,
And at the corner of the street
A lonely cab-horse steams and stamps.
And then the lighting of the lamps.

II

The morning comes to consciousness
Of faint stale smells of beer
From the sawdust-trampled street
With all its muddy feet that press
To early coffee-stands.

With the other masquerades

That time resumes,

One thinks of all the hands

That are raising dingy shades

In a thousand furnished rooms.

III

You tossed a blanket from the bed,

You lay upon your back, and waited;

You dozed, and watched the night revealing

The thousand sordid images

Of which your soul was constituted;

They flickered against the ceiling.

And when all the world came back

And the light crept up between the shutters,

And you heard the sparrows in the gutters,

You had such a vision of the street

As the street hardly understands;

Sitting along the bed's edge, where

You curled the papers from your hair,

Or clasped the yellow soles of feet

In the palms of both soiled hands.

IV

His soul stretched tight across the skies

That fade behind a city block,

Or trampled by insistent feet

At four and five and six o'clock;

And short square fingers stuffing pipes,

And evening newspapers, and eyes

Assured of certain certainties,

The conscience of a blackened street

Impatient to assume the world.

I am moved by fancies that are curled

Around these images, and cling:

The notion of some infinitely gentle

Infinitely suffering thing.

Wipe your hand across your mouth, and laugh;

The worlds revolve like ancient women

Gathering fuel in vacant lots.

Rhapsody on a Windy Night

Twelve o'clock.

Along the reaches of the street

Held in a lunar synthesis,

Whispering lunar incantations

Disolve the floors of memory

And all its clear relations,

Its divisions and precisions,

Every street lamp that I pass

Beats like a fatalistic drum,

And through the spaces of the dark

Midnight shakes the memory

As a madman shakes a dead geranium.

Half-past one,

The street lamp sputtered,

The street lamp muttered,

The street lamp said,

"Regard that woman

Who hesitates toward you in the light of the door

Which opens on her like a grin.

You see the border of her dress

Is torn and stained with sand,

And you see the corner of her eye

Twists like a crooked pin."

The memory throws up high and dry

A crowd of twisted things;

A twisted branch upon the beach

Eaten smooth, and polished

As if the world gave up

The secret of its skeleton,

Stiff and white.

A broken spring in a factory yard,

Rust that clings to the form that the strength has left

Hard and curled and ready to snap.

Half-past two,

The street-lamp said,

"Remark the cat which flattens itself in the gutter,

Slips out its tongue

And devours a morsel of rancid butter."

So the hand of the child, automatic,

Slipped out and pocketed a toy that was running along

the quay.

I could see nothing behind that child's eye.

I have seen eyes in the street

Trying to peer through lighted shutters,

And a crab one afternoon in a pool,

An old crab with barnacles on his back,

Gripped the end of a stick which I held him.

Half-past three,

The lamp sputtered,

The lamp muttered in the dark.

The lamp hummed:

"Regard the moon,

La lune ne garde aucune rancune,

She winks a feeble eye,

She smiles into corners.

She smooths the hair of the grass.

The moon has lost her memory.

A washed-out smallpox cracks her face,

Her hand twists a paper rose,

That smells of dust and old Cologne,

She is alone With all the old nocturnal smells

That cross and cross across her brain.

The reminiscence comes

Of sunless dry geraniums

And dust in crevices,

Smells of chestnuts in the streets

And female smells in shuttered rooms

And cigarettes in corridors

And cocktail smells in bars."

The lamp said,

"Four o'clock,

Here is the number on the door.

Memory!

You have the key,

The little lamp spreads a ring on the stair,

Mount.

The bed is open; the tooth-brush hangs on the wall,

Put your shoes at the door, sleep, prepare for life."

The last twist of the knife.

Morning at the Window

They are rattling breakfast plates in basement kitchens,

And along the trampled edges of the street

I am aware of the damp souls of housemaids

Sprouting despondently at area gates.

The brown waves of fog toss up to me

Twisted faces from the bottom of the street,

And tear from a passer-by with muddy skirts

An aimless smile that hovers in the air

And vanishes along the level of the roofs.

The Boston Evening Transcript

The readers of the Boston Evening Transcript

Sway in the wind like a field of ripe corn.

When evening quickens faintly in the street,

Wakening the appetites of life in some

And to others bringing the Boston Evening Transcript,

I mount the steps and ring the bell, turning

Wearily, as one would turn to nod good-bye to Rochefoucauld,

If the street were time and he at the end of the street,

And I say, "Cousin Harriet, here is the Boston Evening Transcript."

Aunt Helen

Miss Helen Slingsby was my maiden aunt,

And lived in a small house near a fashionable square

Cared for by servants to the number of four.

Now when she died there was silence in heaven

And silence at her end of the street.

The shutters were drawn and the undertaker wiped his feet—

He was aware that this sort of thing had occurred before.

The dogs were handsomely provided for,

But shortly afterwards the parrot died too.

The Dresden clock continued ticking on the mantelpiece,

And the footman sat upon the dining-table

Holding the second housemaid on his knees—

Who had always been so careful while her mistress lived.

Cousin Nancy

Miss Nancy Ellicott Strode across the hills and broke them,

Rode across the hills and broke them—

The barren New England hills—

Riding to hounds

Over the cow-pasture.

Miss Nancy Ellicott smoked

And danced all the modern dances;

And her aunts were not quite sure how they felt about it,

But they knew that it was modern.

Upon the glazen shelves kept watch

Matthew and Waldo, guardians of the faith,

The army of unalterable law.

Mr. Apollinax

When Mr. Apollinax visited the United States

His laughter tinkled among the teacups.

I thought of Fragilion, that shy figure among the birch-trees,

And of Priapus in the shrubbery

Gaping at the lady in the swing.

In the palace of Mrs. Phlaccus, at Professor Channing-Cheetah's

He laughed like an irresponsible foetus.

His laughter was submarine and profound

Like the old man of the sea's

Hidden under coral islands

Where worried bodies of drowned men drift down in the green silence,

Dropping from fingers of surf.

I looked for the head of Mr. Apollinax rolling under a chair

Or grinning over a screen

With seaweed in its hair.

I heard the beat of centaur's hoofs over the hard turf

As his dry and passionate talk devoured the afternoon.

"He is a charming man"—"But after all what did he mean?"—

"His pointed ears... He must be unbalanced,"—

"There was something he said that I might have challenged."

Of dowager Mrs. Phlaccus, and Professor and Mrs. Cheetah

I remember a slice of lemon, and a bitten macaroon.

Hysteria

As she laughed I was aware of becoming involved in her
laughter and being part of it, until her teeth were
only accidental stars with a talent for squad-drill. I
was drawn in by short gasps, inhaled at each momentary
recovery, lost finally in the dark caverns of her
throat, bruised by the ripple of unseen muscles. An
elderly waiter with trembling hands was hurriedly
spreading a pink and white checked cloth over the rusty
green iron table, saying: "If the lady and gentleman
wish to take their tea in the garden, if the lady and
gentleman wish to take their tea in the garden..." I
decided that if the shaking of her breasts could be
stopped, some of the fragments of the afternoon might
be collected, and I concentrated my attention with
careful subtlety to this end.

Conversation Galante

I observe: "Our sentimental friend the moon!

Or possibly (fantastic, I confess)

It may be Prester John's balloon

Or an old battered lantern hung aloft

To light poor travellers to their distress."

  She then: "How you digress!"

And I then: "Some one frames upon the keys

That exquisite nocturne, with which we explain

The night and moonshine; music which we seize

To body forth our vacuity."

  She then: "Does this refer to me?"

  "Oh no, it is I who am inane."

"You, madam, are the eternal humorist,

The eternal enemy of the absolute,

Giving our vagrant moods the slightest twist!

With your air indifferent and imperious

At a stroke our mad poetics to confute—"

  And—"Are we then so serious?"

La Figlia Che Piange

    O quam te memorem Virgo...

Stand on the highest pavement of the stair—

Lean on a garden urn—

Weave, weave the sunlight in your hair—

Clasp your flowers to you with a pained surprise—

Fling them to the ground and turn

With a fugitive resentment in your eyes:

But weave, weave the sunlight in your hair.

So I would have had him leave,

So I would have had her stand and grieve,

So he would have left

As the soul leaves the body torn and bruised,

As the mind deserts the body it has used.

I should find

Some way incomparably light and deft,

Some way we both should understand,

Simple and faithless as a smile and shake of the hand.

She turned away, but with the autumn weather

Compelled my imagination many days,

Many days and many hours:

Her hair over her arms and her arms full of flowers.

And I wonder how they should have been together!

I should have lost a gesture and a pose.

Sometimes these cogitations still amaze

The troubled midnight and the noon's repose.

Made in the USA
Coppell, TX
11 June 2021